Shadows

Shadows
under the Sea

Sally Grindley

BLOOMSBURY

LONDON BERLIN NEW YORK SYDNEY

Bloomsbury Publishing, London, Berlin, New York and Sydney

First published in Great Britain in May 2012 by Bloomsbury Publishing Plc
50 Bedford Square, London, WC1B 3DP

Manufactured and supplied under licence from the Zoological Society of London

Text copyright © Sally Grindley 2012

The moral right of the author has been asserted

Licensed by Bright Group International
www.thebrightagency.com

With thanks to ZSL's conservation team
and *Project Seahorse* by Pamela S. Turner
with photographs by Scott Tuason (Houghton Mifflin Harcourt, 2010)

A CIP catalogue record for this book is available from the British Library

ISBN 978 1 4088 1944 9

MIX
Paper from
responsible sources
FSC
www.fsc.org
FSC® C018072

Typeset by Hewer Text UK Ltd, Edinburgh
Printed in Great Britain by Clays Ltd, St Ives plc, Bungay, Suffolk

1 3 5 7 9 10 8 6 4 2

www.storiesfromthezoo.com
www.bloomsbury.com
www.sallygrindley.co.uk

Chapter 1

'Name the smallest horse in the world,' Peter Brook challenged his two children.

Aesha had just returned from swimming practice. She dumped her bag in the middle of the hall and joined her father in the kitchen. Joe, hearing the sounds of his sister and mother's return, had appeared from upstairs, where he had been doing his homework.

'A pony,' he said.

'Funny, ha, ha!' scoffed Aesha. 'That's not a type of horse — it's just a young horse.'

'No, it's not,' argued Joe. 'A pony is a particular type of horse with a small build. Isn't it, Mum?'

Binti nodded. 'Joe's right, love. You're confusing pony with foal.'

'Shetland, then,' Aesha said sulkily. 'Who cares, anyway?' At thirteen, she was four years older than Joe and didn't like it when he proved her wrong.

'That counts as a pony, and I said pony,' Joe objected.

'You're both wrong.' Their father grinned. 'I'm thinking of something much, much smaller.'

'I know!' cried Joe. 'A seahorse!'

'Correct,' said Peter. 'Go to the top of the class.'

'That's cheating,' Aesha grumbled.

'As my favourite little water baby, I thought you'd be the first to guess.' Peter held a bowl of peanuts out to placate her. 'Now, guess who's been invited to photograph seahorses in the Philippines!'

'And guess who's going with him!' said Binti.

'The Queen,' Aesha suggested.

Her father pretended to cuff her.

'You, Dad? And you, Mum?' Joe questioned.

'Anyone else going?' Aesha asked cautiously.

'Pick your swimming bag up off the floor if you want the answer to be yes,' Binti instructed.

'We're *all* going to the Philippines for four weeks over the summer holidays,' Peter confirmed the minute Aesha had emptied the contents of the swimming bag into the wash and put it away.

'Cool!' said Joe.

'It'll be rather hot, actually!' said his father.

'Even better!' Aesha joined in. She hated the cold, and even though she had enjoyed their recent trip to eastern Russia, where her mother had been invited to work with tiger experts, she much preferred the idea of going somewhere hot.

'What will you do while we're there, Mum?' Joe asked.

'I hope to learn a little more about seahorses,' she replied. 'They're not something I've ever had to deal with. However, since more and more people are keeping them in aquaria –

because they're cute – it might be as well if I were better informed.'

Binti was an international wildlife vet who worked locally with sick animals, and regularly travelled overseas to lend her expertise where it was needed.

'I bet the seahorses don't like being kept in aquaria very much,' said Joe.

'Unless you're a real expert, they're very tricky to look after,' replied Binti. 'Seahorses are fussy eaters and get sick and stressed very easily, especially if they don't have somewhere to hide or are put in with other fish that take their food.'

'People are so dumb,' said Aesha. 'Why do they have to turn every animal into a pet?'

'It's one of the reasons they're becoming endangered,' Binti said.

'What, people?' Peter grinned.

'Bad joke, Dad,' said Aesha. 'Will we be able to go snorkelling?'

He nodded. 'Of course – you'll be like a

couple of beetles scuttling around on top of the water.'

'How long is the flight to the Philippines?' Joe wanted to know.

'It's around twelve hours to Hong Kong, and then another two and a half hours to Cebu,' said Binti.

Joe groaned. 'I hate long flights – they're so boring, and I can never get to sleep.'

'That's because you spend your time imagining that everyone else is up to no good.' Peter laughed.

'That's not true,' Joe protested. 'Just because I thought someone on a plane was a smuggler once . . .'

'When are we going?' Aesha asked.

'Two days after you break up from school. You children just don't know how lucky you are.'

Joe looked at his father. He thought he probably *did* know how lucky they were – his friends told him often enough. It would have been easy to think that everyone travelled to far-flung corners of the world on a regular basis considering his family's lifestyle, but his friends assured him that wasn't the case.

'Poor Foggy will be off to the doggery again, I suppose,' Joe said, pushing his bottom lip out sadly.

'Poor Foggy will be off to Waggy Tails Boarding Kennels, as usual, where he'll be seriously pampered and spoilt, leaving your mother and me teetering on the edge of bankruptcy.'

'As an endangered species, I'm sure the seahorses will be very grateful for any sacrifices Foggy makes on their behalf,' Binti replied, smiling.

Chapter 2

Since his father's announcement, Joe had been counting down the days to their trip and now, the day before they were due to leave, he was amazed to discover that the Philippines were an archipelago of over seven thousand islands in the Pacific Ocean. He hadn't given it much thought until then.

'Only four thousand are lived on,' his father told him. 'The rest are too small or are uninhabitable.'

'Will we stay on just one of them?'

'We'll stay for several days on Jandayan Island, which is where many of the studies on seahorses are being carried out, and then we'll go island-hopping.'

'Cool!' said Joe.

Binti explained that there were at least forty species of seahorse in the world.

'The largest is the big-belly seahorse, which is about the size of a banana, while the smallest is Denise's pygmy, which is about the size of a pine nut.'

'I can tell you something about seahorses too,' said Aesha. 'It's the male that gives birth to the babies and he carries them in his pouch.'

'Quite right,' Binti agreed. 'Depending on the species, he can be pregnant from nine to forty-five days, and may have between five and two thousand babies in his pouch.'

'Two thousand!' Joe exclaimed.

'I know something else,' said Aesha proudly. 'Seahorses mate for life.'

'Ah, isn't that nice,' said Peter. 'Just like your mum and me. Though when she gives me one of her scary looks, I wonder if I haven't made a big mistake.'

Binti gave him a scary look and chased him with a tea towel. Joe joined in, pulling the worst face he could, and Foggy, their schnauzer, woken by the excitement, scurried round Peter's legs, barking loudly.

'I knew it! My son's taking after his mother, and even the dog's against me,' Peter cried dramatically. 'I bet a big-belly seahorse doesn't have to put up with such treatment. I'll have to retire to my shed for a bit of peace and quiet.'

'A seahorse doesn't have a shed to retire to,' Aesha observed.

'More like a stable!' Joe chortled. 'Ha!'

'You're all mad,' said Binti, 'and I'll be hopping mad if you don't hurry up and finish packing.'

'Do you mean island-hopping mad?' Joe said, grinning.

'Ha, funny, ha,' said Aesha. 'You and Dad tell the worst jokes.'

'Nobody would think we were going away for a month tomorrow morning from the state of your rooms,' said Binti in exasperation. 'Now move!'

'It's that scary face again,' Peter said.

Binti picked up a broom and swept them out of the kitchen.

Joe ran to his bedroom, shoved his model-making kit under the bed, grabbed his underpants, T-shirts and shorts from the drawers and dumped them in the case Binti had left out for him. He took his camera from the shelf, wrapped it in a towel and placed it carefully in a corner of the case. Then he picked up his flip-flops and a pair of sandals and threw them in on top. He could hear Aesha complaining that her suitcase was too small to accommodate everything she needed, and his father replying that she wouldn't require her ball gown and tiara where they were going.

Joe was incredibly excited. He had been on plenty of trips with his parents before, but this one promised to be particularly fascinating, and he would have plenty of opportunities to take photographs like his father. He loved travelling on boats and he had never snorkelled before, so that was something else to look forward to. There was also something very appealing about seahorses that made him eager to see them in their natural environment. He laid his brand new flippers and snorkel mask in the suitcase, hoping that this was going to be his best adventure yet.

Chapter 3

Joe bagged the window seat on the flight from Heathrow to Hong Kong. He loved looking out as the plane left the ground and everything grew smaller and smaller. He was amused for a while by a young Filipino girl who kept popping up from the seat in front, gazing over the top of it, bright-eyed and mischievous, then ducking down again. Peter encouraged her by pulling hilarious faces, but the game stopped when she fell fast asleep, sprawled across her mother's lap. Joe watched a film, played card games with Binti, and read some of his book, which was about orphan children living on the streets.

'The kids in this story are so poor, Mum, the only way they can get anything to eat is to search through people's rubbish for something to sell.' Joe was indignant that anyone should have to do that.

'I'm afraid it's like that in many parts of the world, and I agree that it's terrible. The Philippines is one of the poorest countries in the world, and lots of children live on the streets in the cities.'

Joe was shocked. He had imagined they were going somewhere full of happiness and sunshine and laughter. He supposed the reason he had thought that was because they had packed T-shirts and shorts and were planning to go snorkelling and island-hopping. It had all sounded very idyllic.

'Is that why seahorses are endangered?' he asked. 'Is it because people sell them to make money to live?'

'It's partly that,' Binti agreed, 'although lots of different things usually combine to cause problems for an endangered species. It's very important for local people to be involved in saving the seahorses, which is why the experts in the field are working very closely with local communities.'

'Like in Russia, with the tigers?'

Binti nodded. 'Without the support of the locals, conservationists fight a losing battle.'

Joe nodded. He had already learnt first-hand how teams of Russians had been trained to patrol areas where the Amur tiger roamed, in order to prevent hunting and poaching.

'It's no different back home, you know,' Binti continued. 'There are plenty of endangered species in England. They may not be as high profile as tigers and rhinos, but that doesn't make them less important. And again, local communities are encouraged to get involved in helping to save them.'

Joe closed his eyes and wondered if there were any endangered species in the area where they lived. He hadn't heard of any, but he could think of a few species he would be happy to see disappear, like daddy-long-legs and cockroaches – and his maths teacher. He didn't think anyone would rally to save his maths teacher.

'Penny for them,' Joe heard his father saying. 'You were grinning all over your face.'

'I was thinking about Mr Gregory.'

'Well, that's nothing to smile about.' His father laughed. 'You hate maths and Mr Gregory is your worst nightmare. I can't believe you're taking them on holiday with you.'

'I wish both of them were extinct!' Joe grinned again.

'Poor Mr Gregory,' said Peter. 'I'm sure somebody somewhere would miss him.'

'Were you good at maths at school, Dad?' Joe asked.

'Hopeless,' said Peter. 'You take after your old man in that direction, I'm afraid. Your mum's much better.'

Joe closed his eyes again. This time his mind drifted away on images of his family swimming like fish in a warm sea, surrounded by seahorses and other marine creatures, and accepted as guardians of their environment. Even the sharks were friendly, swimming alongside them, nudging them with their noses every so often . . .

When a voice eventually found its way through the water, telling him to fasten his seat belt, he ignored it first of all, thinking that this instruction couldn't apply to him. He felt someone leaning across him and, as he surfaced for air, he heard someone say that they were coming in to land.

Chapter 4

The flight from Hong Kong to Cebu passed very quickly. Joe and his family were refreshed from an overnight stay at a hotel in Hong Kong, and no sooner had they boarded the flight, it seemed, than they were being told to prepare for landing. Much to Joe's delight, the final part of their journey was to be by sea.

They reached the harbour-side by midday and were shown to their boat. Joe thought it was the weirdest thing he had ever seen! It was very narrow and pointed at both ends, and had several bent wooden poles sticking out from each side, making it look like a giant

water boatman. There were four other passengers already sitting under the canopy in the
middle, together with a pig and two cockerels
that kept fighting.

'We're not going on there, are we?' Aesha
was horrified.

'Unless you've learnt to walk on water, yes,'
Peter replied.

'It's cool!' said Joe.

As soon as he had been helped on board, he
made for the front and beckoned his family to
join him.

'We can see everything from here,' he said
excitedly.

It was a beautiful warm day. While they
waited for the boat to depart, Joe peered over
the side to see if he could catch his first glimpse
of marine life. A shoal of small brown fish flashed
by, so close to the water's surface that he could
have touched them had the sides of the boat
been lower. He wondered if there were seahorses
deeper down. It gave him a funny feeling to

think that a whole world of activity was going on unseen below them.

There was also a whole world of activity on the seafront as the boat's engine started up. Crowds of children had gathered and were waving cheerfully at them. Binti waved back and Joe and Aesha joined in. Beside them, their father was preparing his video camera. Joe wished he had taken his own camera from his suitcase, which had been stowed on a luggage rack underneath a pile of others. '*One of the secrets of being a successful photographer,*' Peter had told him more than once, '*is being ready to snap when the unexpected happens.*'

'What are you going to photograph?' Joe asked.

'Children who are as poor as church mice with great big smiles on their faces,' Peter replied. 'No mobiles, no laptops, no shoes on their feet, but look at them.'

The children were even happier when they realised they were being filmed. Joe couldn't help but laugh at their antics as they paraded up and down. The boat began to move away and the children followed along the harbour path, cheering wildly, until it headed out to sea and left them in its wake.

Joe felt exhilarated now. The wind buffeted his face and the spray coated him with salt as the boat sped across the water. He didn't want to stop – he wanted it to head for the horizon and keep on going.

'Don't you wish we had a speedboat, Dad?' he shouted above the noise of the engine.

'It wouldn't be much good in the middle of Surrey,' his father shouted back.

They passed one island after another, and each time Joe expected them to stop, but it was nearly three hours later before they approached an island and the boat began to slow down.

'There are more of those weird-looking boats,' Joe said, pointing to the shore, where there were rows of very narrow colourful hulls, each with the same curious arrangement of poles on either side.

'They're called *bancas*,' said Peter. 'Those particular ones are fishing boats, I should think. The network of poles act as stabilisers so that they don't capsize.'

As they drew closer to the landing stage, another crowd of children gathered, some of them pushing and shoving to be first to greet the strangers who were visiting their island.

'It makes you feel like a Very Important Person, doesn't it?' said Binti.

'I *am* a Very Important Person,' said Peter, adopting a lofty air.

'Only in your own head, Dad,' scoffed Aesha.

The boat's engine cut out completely and the captain allowed the boat to drift to its mooring. One of the crew threw a thick rope to a man on the landing stage, who quickly secured it round a mooring post and then beckoned to the passengers to disembark.

Joe looked beyond the crowd of children to

glean some idea of the place where they would be spending the next few days before going to a bigger island called Bohol. It was very green, he thought, with lots of palm trees, and there were numerous small shacks dotted around. He wondered where his family would be staying and hoped it wouldn't be somewhere too grand. He wanted to live like the village children, who were looking at him curiously as he stepped off the boat. Suddenly he felt rather conspicuous, and wished his mother hadn't bought him a new pair of trainers.

'*Mabuhay*,' one young girl said to him, smiling brightly. 'Welcome.'

Joe blushed. 'Thank you,' he replied.

'Peter? Peter Brook?' a voice called.

A blonde woman in her thirties came forward to greet them. She held out her hand to Peter.

'Angela Butler from the seahorse project,' she informed him. 'Welcome to the island of Jandayan and the village of Handumon. I'm delighted our work is attracting so much attention.'

'And I'm delighted to have the opportunity of photographing such extraordinary creatures,' said Peter.

'You must be Binti,' Angela continued, holding her hand out again. 'I've heard a lot about you from colleagues of mine.'

'It's very kind of you to allow me to follow your work while my husband's here,' said Binti. 'These are our children, Aesha and Joe.'

Angela welcomed them warmly. 'We've made room for you all in the staff house,' she said. 'It's basic, but clean and comfortable, and it's one of the few places in the village with electricity. There's no running water, though, I'm afraid.'

'Don't worry about that.' Binti smiled. 'We're used to basic, aren't we?' She aimed the question at Joe and Aesha.

Joe nodded his head firmly, but Aesha looked less certain.

Angela summoned a driver to transport their suitcases to the staff house by motorbike. 'We can walk,' she said. 'It's not far.'

She led them along a dusty road. Chickens scattered to the right and left, squawking loudly. Dogs lying by the roadside raised sleepy eyelids, briefly took in the passing procession, then closed them again. Joe was amused to find that the children were still following them, chattering loudly, several of them calling 'Hello' in English and giggling coyly among themselves.

'They love having visitors,' said Angela. 'They'll be endlessly curious about you.'

'Will they mind if I take photos of them?' Peter asked.

'They'll *love* you to take their photos.' Angela laughed. 'It'll make them feel like rock stars.'

There were pigs tethered outside some of the houses. Joe chuckled at the way they were snuffling around in the dirt for something to eat.

'Pigs are a prized possession here,' said Angela. 'They're a rare source of meat. The islanders live mostly on rice and whatever fish they've been able to catch. Even then, they take the best of their catch to market and keep the less desirable fish for themselves.'

Joe hoped that if he were served fish it wouldn't be too bony. He couldn't stand bony fish.

They turned a corner and reached the staff house. It was a long, rectangular building supported by a number of concrete pillars. Its high, thatched roof overhung the walls, which were made of intricately woven palm leaves around a wooden framework and wide windows. One side of the roof virtually reached the ground.

'Welcome to the home of the seahorse project,' said Angela. 'I hope you'll enjoy your stay.'

She showed them into a big communal room, where two young Filipino men were working at a large wooden table, one using a laptop, the other plotting something on a map. On one wall was a blackboard covered with chalked notes. In a corner stood an old-fashioned hi-fi system.

'This is Rey and Carl, who help us to monitor the seahorse populations. They'll be diving with you when you take your photos, Peter.' Angela completed the introductions and led them along a corridor to their rooms. 'I hope you and Joe won't mind sharing,' she said to Aesha as she opened the door to a room with sleeping mats side by side on the floor. 'I'm afraid you'll have to share the mosquito net as well.'

'I prefer Joe to mosquitoes – just,' said Aesha, looking rather dubiously at the sleeping mats, 'so I guess I'll cope.'

'Huh!' said Joe. 'I think I might prefer mosquitoes.'

'Not in the middle of the night when you hear their continuous buzzing and know they're searching for a way to get at you.' Angela laughed. 'And I'm afraid there is a lot of rain,' she added, as heavy drops fell past the open window.

She left them to unpack. Aesha made no attempt to unload her clothes into the rickety cupboard in the corner of the room. Instead, she stood by the window and groaned loudly.

'I can't believe we've got to sleep on the floor,' she grumbled. 'And Dad said we were going somewhere hot, not wet.'

Joe refused to be disheartened. 'We'll be in the water a lot of the time,' he said, 'so it won't matter if it rains!'

Chapter 5

It turned out to be only a shower. The sun quickly returned to dry up the moisture, leaving the ground and the air steaming.

'It's so humid!' Aesha exclaimed as they set off for a walk later in the afternoon. 'I can't imagine having to live here.'

'You wanted hot,' said her father.

'Not this hot!' replied Aesha.

'You'd be used to it if you lived here,' said Binti. 'And you'd adjust your pace of life accordingly – you don't see the locals dashing around like we do at home.'

It was true, Joe acknowledged. Those who

were outside were going about their chores in a leisurely fashion, almost as if they too were on holiday. At home, everyone would be jumping in and out of cars, dashing off to football or swimming or school or shopping. He wondered if that would all change if the weather in England suddenly became hot and humid. He thought he would want to live by the sea if it did.

'When are we going to look at the seahorses?' he asked.

'In the middle of the night,' said Peter.

'I meant seriously, Dad,' Joe reproached him.

'In the middle of the night,' Peter repeated. 'That's when the seahorses and other sea creatures spring to life.'

'But how will we see anything?' asked Joe.

'I believe the locals use a very simple gas lamp,' said Peter.

'So we're going to walk into the sea in the middle of the night carrying a gas lamp?' Aesha was struggling to grasp her father's meaning.

'We'll be going in a *banca* with a gas lamp attached to it,' he explained.

'Cool!' said Joe. This definitely sounded like an amazing adventure.

'We'll make an exploratory trip first of all. I shall be diving, but you'll be able to snorkel at the same time, once you've had some practice. And if you're good, I'll bring you up some tasty titbits from the seabed.'

'Like an old boot, if I know you, Dad.' Aesha snorted.

'I can't believe we're going to go snorkelling in the middle of the night,' said Joe. 'Are we going tonight?'

'Not tonight!' said Binti. 'We'll need our sleep tonight after such a long journey.'

'Oh,' said Joe, pouting. 'I'm not tired.'

'You will be,' Binti replied, and as if she had woven some sort of magic, Joe found himself yawning.

'Ha!' said Peter. 'You'll be asleep before we get to the beach.'

'No, I won't,' retorted Joe. 'I'll race you there!'

He sped off down the path, his father hot on his tail. Several village children, sensing there was some fun to be had, ran after them, shouting and laughing. Peter began to zigzag from side to side, the children copying his every move.

'You're completely mad, Dad!' Aesha called after him.

Joe reached the sand and found a large piece of seaweed. He hid it behind his back, adopted an innocent look and stood waiting for his father to catch up.

'What took you so long?' he said, grinning, when Peter arrived, out of breath. 'Poor Dad. You look worn out.'

Before his father knew what was happening, Joe rushed towards him and shoved the seaweed down his shorts, much to the amusement of the Filipino children, who stared wide-eyed and then giggled uncontrollably.

'Ha, ha, Dad,' called Aesha. 'You didn't see that one coming!'

'You wait,' said Peter, putting on a sinister voice as he pulled the seaweed from his shorts. 'I shall have my revenge, and you won't know when it will hit you.'

'There's a boat full of seaweed over there,' said Aesha.

'Don't give me ideas.' Peter smirked.

'What would anyone want with a boat full of seaweed?' questioned Joe.

'Some of it will be eaten. Apparently it's delicious raw with vinegar, onions and chilli,' Binti replied. 'A lot will be sold. It's used in all sorts of things, like make-up, toothpaste, ice cream –'

'Seaweed ice cream?' Joe interrupted. 'Yuck!'

'The ice cream isn't seaweed flavoured.' Binti laughed. 'Seaweed extract is used in it as a thickening agent.'

They wandered over to the *banca* that was piled high with seaweed. Peter got out his camera and took a number of photographs from different angles, while the Filipino children did everything they could to appear in them. Joe was cross with himself that in his excitement to get out and explore he had left his camera behind again. He would have liked to take photographs of the children trying to get into his father's shots.

'What your name?' one of the boys asked him out of the blue.

'Joe,' he replied, and began to fiddle shyly with a rope that was hanging out of the *banca*.

'Me, Dario,' said the boy, pointing to himself. 'You play basketball with us?'

Joe blushed and looked to his mother to answer for him.

'Joe would love to play basketball with you,' Binti said, smiling. 'Perhaps tomorrow?'

Dario nodded. 'Tomorrow is good.'

Joe wasn't at all sure he wanted to play basketball with strangers. He wasn't particularly good at sport and Dario was taller and looked older than him. At the same time, he liked the idea of having a friend on the island, especially a friend he could share adventures with.

Chapter 6

By the time they had finished their walk along the beach, eaten and watched the sun go down, Joe could scarcely keep his eyes open.

'What a perfect end to the day,' Binti sighed, yawning herself. 'That's one of the most beautiful sunsets I've ever seen.'

'There's definitely a lot to be said for going back to nature,' said Peter. 'We scarcely notice the sun setting at home.'

'That's because there are too many buildings in the way,' Aesha said.

'Ah, but would we take any notice if there

weren't?' Peter commented. 'We're always too busy looking down.'

'They're never as spectacular as this anyway,' said Aesha. 'We're spoilt now – no sunset will ever be able to match up to this.'

Joe saw a crab scuttle across the sand. If he hadn't been so tired, he would have run after it. Instead, he lay back, his arms behind his head, and stared up at the sky. He was on an island far, far from home – the sort of place where adventures happened, or at least they did in books. In books, treasure was buried on islands and pirates moored their ships just off the shore. Strange people and animals lived on imaginary islands, and visitors often got lost in their hazard-ous landscapes or became ill with deadly fevers. Joe wondered about the people of Jandayan – about the fishermen and the seaweed farmers, about the women he saw sweeping outside their houses and others who stood washing clothes or cooking on open fires. They seemed friendly, but what were they really like?

And Dario. What was he like? Did he have some hidden reason for asking Joe to play basketball with him, or was he just being kind to a young boy who might appreciate some company from someone closer to his age?

Anyway, surely there can't be a basketball court on the island? Joe considered. He was a little anxious about going with him, but he was curious too. With Dario he thought he would find out a lot more about real life on the island. *With Dario, I'm far more likely to have an adventure.*

Then he scolded himself because he decided that nothing could be more of an adventure than searching for seahorses and other marine creatures in the middle of the night. He had read books about children having secret midnight feasts, but night-time snorkelling would be far more exciting. As for basketball, he could play that anywhere.

'Time for bed, sleepyhead.' A voice broke through his thoughts.

Peter helped him to his feet. 'You were muttering something about baskets,' he said. 'Those seaweed farmers have obviously made a big impression on you.'

Joe grinned sheepishly. 'I don't think I'd want it as a job,' he said.

On the way back to the staff house, they came across a large wooden noticeboard with a map of the island painted on it. To Joe's surprise, among the few places named on the map, which included the school and the church, was a basketball court, though it wasn't clear exactly where it was on the island.

'There you are, Joe,' said Binti, pointing at the list. 'This might be a tiny village, but it obviously takes its basketball very seriously.'

Joe groaned. 'I'm going to be too busy taking photos to play,' he said.

'Even I won't be taking photos all day every day,' said Peter. 'Especially if it keeps raining,' he added, as the heavens opened again. 'Race you home!'

If it keeps raining, I won't be able to play basketball anyway, Joe thought, haring after his father.

It rained all night, but by morning the sun was shining hotly again. Joe woke early and went outside. Drops of water fell non-stop from the palm trees, one of them landing plumb on the top of his head and making him jump almost as much as he might have done if it were a palm nut. He wandered through the grounds of the staff house and came across a large concreted area containing several wooden benches and covered with a thatched roof. It was only when he had stepped up on to the base that he realised someone else was there.

'You're up early, Joe.' Angela's head popped round the side of a noticeboard on which she had been writing.

'I was hot,' said Joe shyly. 'And I never sleep late. Aesha does – Dad says she can sleep for England.'

'You're like me,' said Angela. 'I hate to see the day being wasted. Talking of which, how would you like to go on a boat trip today? I thought we could take you all around the Marine Protected Areas and the mangroves.'

Joe nodded eagerly. 'Will we go on one of those *banca* things?'

Angela laughed. 'Yes, we'll go on one of those *banca* things.'

'What exactly are mangroves?' he asked.

'Ah, now there's a subject,' Angela replied. 'Basically, they're dense areas of low trees and shrubs that have adapted to grow in saltwater. The trees and shrubs have lots of roots that act as props to support them and they form a tangled mass, mostly underwater, in which all sorts of marine creatures live. Without them, we'd lose most of our fish and many other creatures as well.'

Joe took in what she was saying. 'Fish stocks are low all over the world, aren't they?' he asked. He had heard something about it on the news back home, but found it difficult to believe that, given the size of the world's oceans, there could be any shortage.

'Overfishing goes on everywhere,' Angela agreed. 'The human population is exploding, and more and more people are eating fish because it's a healthy food, but the poor old fish can't reproduce quickly enough.'

Joe made up his mind there and then that he would stop being fussy about fish and eat every last morsel that was put on his plate from that point onwards.

Chapter 7

Joe was impatient for his family to be up and about when he returned to the staff house.

'Hurry up,' he growled at Aesha. 'Half the day's gone already and everyone else has been up for hours.'

'Just because you've got ants in your pants, it doesn't mean we all have to get up at the crack of dawn,' said Aesha.

'What's the point of staying in bed all day when you're in a different country,' Joe countered. 'We might never come here again.'

'It's only eight o'clock, Joe,' said Aesha. 'It's not as if we're missing out on anything.'

'You've missed out on helping to get the *banca* ready. I helped put the canopy up and load the bottles of water on board.'

Aesha looked unimpressed, but Joe had felt very important working alongside Angela and Rey while the rest of his family slept. They had talked to him about the seahorse project and how vital it was to keep the local population involved in protecting the species.

'Rey used to collect and sell seahorses,' Angela told him, 'but when he realised their numbers were dropping disastrously, he began to work with us to find alternative ways for local people to earn an income.'

Rey nodded enthusiastically. 'Now, my wife, she makes baskets, and I work with Ma'am Angela to stop the dynamite and save the coral.'

'Did you know that some people use dyna-mite to blast fish out of the water?' Joe asked his parents as they headed towards the *banca* at last.

Binti nodded. 'It's a way of catching a lot of fish quickly.'

'But how?' demanded Aesha. 'Doesn't it blow the fish to pieces?'

Joe was delighted to have caught her attention. 'It blows some of them to pieces and it kills the coral reef, but it makes it easy to collect the fish that aren't destroyed from the surface of the water,' he explained.

'I can't believe people can be so stupid.' Aesha frowned.

'It's very short-sighted,' said Binti. 'Once a reef is damaged, it takes a very long time to recover, and all the creatures that depend upon it as well. The short-term gain for dynamite fishermen results in long-term problems for everyone else. But you can't always blame them – not if all they're trying to do is feed their children. I'd probably do the same if there were no other option.'

'I can't quite see you going that far.' Peter linked arms with her as they walked over the sand.

They reached the *banca*. Joe felt a sense of ownership as they helped push it into the water, and he made sure to climb on board first in order to claim the seat he wanted.

'Will it be cooler away from land?' Aesha asked, wiping the back of her hand across her forehead.

'Are you suffering?' Angela smiled sympathetically. 'It is horribly sticky today, isn't it? There should be a bit of a breeze over the sea, but we won't be travelling fast enough to create our own. You can always slip over the side into the water to cool off.'

'Not now!' Joe butted in, anxious to be on his way.

'Of course not now.' Aesha scowled at him.

At that very moment Rey managed to coax the engine into life and the boat began to move forward, gradually picking up speed.

'Hold on to your hats then – we're off!' called Angela above the noise of the engine.

This is so exciting! thought Joe as the boat bumped up and down on the waves. *I hope we see some dolphins.*

'Will we see any dolphins?' he asked his father, who was sitting on the bench opposite, fiddling with his camera, which prompted Joe to bring his own camera out.

'I'd love to swim with dolphins,' said Aesha. 'That would be so cool.'

'You're such a good swimmer, they'd be queuing up to swim with *you*.' Peter laughed.

'I'm afraid there aren't any dolphins in this particular area,' Angela informed them. 'But you might be lucky enough to see them when you visit some of the other islands,' she added when she saw Joe's look of disappointment.

They headed out to sea, turning towards a large wooden hut on stilts. Angela explained that it was a guardhouse, built to enable a constant watch to be kept on the Marine Protected Area.

'It's the job of several specially trained fish wardens to man it day and night,' said Angela. 'They keep an eye out for any unusual or illegal activity.'

Joe thought it would be quite good fun

spending a night there, though it would be scary as well, listening to the strange noises that seemed to start up the moment darkness fell. He had been comforted to have Aesha sleeping on the mat next to him the previous night, even if she did keep complaining that he was a fidget.

'You mean they have to stay there all night just watching?' His sister was aghast. 'How boring is that!'

'They find ways to entertain themselves,' said Angela. 'They have a radio and play cards and cook meals there.'

As she spoke, a man and a woman appeared on the balcony surrounding the guardhouse and waved at them.

'We've made their day bringing visitors to see them.' Angela waved back and exchanged a few words with them in Cebuano, the local dialect. 'They're excited too about seeing a whale shark early this morning,' she reported.

'Cool!' cried Joe. 'I wish I'd seen it.'

'You'll have to spend the night out here then,'

said Peter. He was only joking, but to Joe it sounded like the best idea in the world.

'I wish I could,' he said.

'Don't worry, Joe.' Angela smiled at him. 'We'll make sure you have plenty of excitement while you're here.'

Chapter 8

The Brook family and Angela spent the day touring the Marine Protected Area, which was marked out with buoys, while Angela talked about its history.

'The area measures fifty hectares altogether and was set up in 1995,' she informed them. 'It's part of a very rare double reef – there are only six in the world. Because of decades of illegal fishing, only five per cent of the Philippines' reefs are in good condition.'

'Is this the only Marine Protected Area?' Binti asked.

'Some five hundred have been set up over the

past thirty years, but many have been hampered by bad practice and weak management. Ours is one of the best in the Philippines,' Angela added proudly. 'Further along the reef, though nothing to do with us, two enormous religious statues have been erected eighteen metres below the surface to deter illegal fishermen and remind them of their duty to preserve the world's wonders.'

'What an extraordinary idea!' said Binti.

'We need extraordinary ideas to conserve our planet,' Angela said, nodding.

'I like it!' said Peter. 'I'll have to make a special dive trip to photograph them.'

Joe couldn't wait to find out what was going on underneath the gently rolling waves, but he was more interested in the marine creatures than in two giant statues. When Angela suggested to Rey that they stop for a swim, he stood up so fast that he lost his balance and nearly toppled over the side.

'Steady,' said Peter, grabbing his arm. 'It might be better to take your shorts off first!'

'There aren't sharks or anything, are there?' Aesha asked.

'There's nothing that will bother you here,' Angela replied.

One after the other they dived overboard. Joe watched enviously as Aesha knifed her way through the waves, scarcely creating any disturbance, and was soon a long distance from them. He paddled around, keeping close to the *banca* and occasionally hanging on to the outrigging while he put his head underwater to look for fish.

The sea's so warm, he thought, remembering outings to Brighton, where they had hardly dared put a toe in the water for fear of hypothermia. *It's like being in a bath*.

After their swim, they clambered back on board the *banca* and headed towards the mangroves.

'Keep your eyes peeled,' said Angela as they drew nearer. 'If you're very, very lucky you might spot a monitor lizard.'

'What else?' asked Joe eagerly, immediately scouring the tops of the trees.

'Dugongs have been spotted very occasionally among the seagrass,' said Angela, 'and there used to be mangrove sharks.'

Now Joe didn't know whether to look up or down; he was sure he would miss something whichever direction he chose. Rey cut the engine on the *banca* and allowed it to drift right up close so that they could see the dense mangrove roots, some of them surrounded by thick brown mud.

'It's like a dirty smelly swamp in places,' said Aesha, wrinkling her nose.

'You'd be surprised how many creatures are living in those dirty smelly swamps.' Angela laughed. 'And you'd be surprised how many products, like medicines and alcohol, have some sort of origin in mangroves. Not to mention the mangroves' importance in preventing soil erosion and protecting the shoreline.'

Joe peered through the water, desperate to see a turtle or a shark, even though Angela had said it was extremely unlikely, then looked back up at the treetops. Peter had loaded his camera and was beginning to take one shot after another.

'What are you photographing, Dad?' Joe asked, fumbling with his own camera case.

'Birdlife,' Peter responded. 'There are so many different species up there.'

'Ah, now if you were to see a Philippine cockatoo that would be a coup,' said Angela. 'They're critically endangered.'

Joe hurried to focus his camera on the trees and wished he had a zoom lens as powerful as his father's.

'How do you keep still when the boat's wobbling?' he asked.

'It's all about using your stomach muscles to help you balance,' replied Peter.

'Joe hasn't got any stomach muscles,' said Aesha.

'I do!' Joe protested.

He lowered his camera and scowled at his sister. As he did, he spotted something silvery leave the waves a short distance behind her, sail in an arc through the air and dive back into the water. He gasped when two similar shapes followed the first.

'Flying fish! I saw flying fish!' he cried excitedly. He raised his camera, focused it and pressed the shutter button just as one of the fish leapt again.

'Where?' Aesha demanded, turning round quickly.

'There were three of them,' Joe insisted. 'Over there. I got a photo – look.'

'Ah.' Angela scrutinized the camera screen. 'Those are sailfish. Look at the long, pointed spears on their heads.'

'Well done, Joe,' said Peter. 'That's what happens when you're prepared.'

They all gazed long and hard in the direction Joe had been facing when he took his photograph. Joe willed the sailfish to show themselves again, but to no avail.

'Never mind.' Angela smiled. 'Hopefully we'll see some more during your stay.'

Chapter 9

There was a large group of children kicking a ball around on the beach when the family returned to Handumon.

'Aren't they lucky to be able to play out here when school's finished?' commented Binti.

'Why aren't they on holiday like us?' asked Joe.

'School terms are different in different parts of the world,' Angela explained. 'Children don't go to school here in midsummer – around April and May – when it's too hot.'

'It's too hot now!' exclaimed Aesha. 'I'm going for a swim to cool down.'

Joe was just thinking about doing the same thing when he spotted Dario heading towards them, the ball under his arm.

'Hello, Ma'am,' he said to Angela, beaming. 'You have good day?'

'We've had a great day, thank you, Dario,' she replied. She turned to Joe and his family. 'Dario is one of my best helpers, and I can rely on him to promote our work, especially among the youngsters.'

'Too much fishing, we go hungry,' he said. 'We play basketball now. You play too, Joe?'

Some of the other children came over and searched Joe's face eagerly.

'Go on, Joe. They're dying for you to join them,' said Peter.

'You'll be quite safe,' Angela encouraged him. 'Dario will look after you well.'

Reluctantly, Joe nodded his head and was quickly surrounded by the other children, who jostled with each other to be by his side.

I just hope they don't expect me to be any good!

he thought to himself as they set off along a winding track away from the village.

As soon as they had left the last of the houses behind, they came to a clearing where a large area of concrete had been laid. It was marked out with lines that had mostly worn away, and at each end stood a rickety-looking wooden post topped with a rusty ring and splintered backboard.

Dario divided the children into teams, picking Joe to be with him and indicating that he should take the jump ball. A taller boy from the other team faced off against Joe in the centre circle. Dario threw the ball in the air, Joe tried to tap it but missed, and the other boy passed it on. For a while Joe was all fingers and thumbs and two left feet, but with Dario's encouragement he began to enjoy himself. He wasn't as good as the other boys, who played with great skill and who knew each other so well that they could anticipate each other's moves, but they went out of their way to involve him. They even helped him score a goal, by allowing him a free run and making no attempt to block him before he reached the basket. He took a shot and was amazed when it found its way through the hoop.

Joe was sorry when a heavy rain shower sent them all scuttling for shelter under the nearby palm trees, but he was tired and hungry too. The other boys stood there chatting, mostly in Cebuano, and it made him feel like an outsider again, even though Dario tried to interpret. Joe was just about to say that he should be going back to the staff house when two men appeared and walked straight across the basketball court. They were both carrying backpacks and talking animatedly. They didn't notice the boys at first, but when they heard one of them laugh they stopped and looked round. Joe thought they seemed annoyed, but then they waved briefly and hurried on their way.

'Do you know them?' he asked Dario.

Dario shook his head. 'I never see them before.'

The other boys agreed that they were strangers. Joe was surprised that they weren't suspicious of the men, but they paid them no more attention as they gave up on the game of basketball and set off home.

'You play next time?' Dario asked when they reached the staff house.

Joe nodded. He was soaked through and rivulets of water ran from his hair down his face, but he was pleased to be asked to play again. 'It was fun – thank you,' he said.

He watched as his new friends splashed their way through the puddles to their own homes before making his way inside. Everyone was gathered in the dining area.

'Now that's what I call a drowned rat!' his father said when he saw him.

'Poor Joe,' said Binti. 'You're soaking wet.'

Joe shrugged. 'I don't mind! I scored a goal and they want me to play with them again.'

'That's great, Joe,' said Angela. 'I'm glad you're enjoying yourself.'

Joe saw that fish and rice were on the menu. He stuck to his resolve to eat every last piece of fish flesh that was put on his plate. It wasn't difficult. That evening, he was so hungry after the day's exertions that it wouldn't have surprised him if he had eaten the skin and bones as well.

Later, as they were preparing for bed, Joe remembered the two men.

What were they doing? he wondered. *Why did they look annoyed when they saw us?*

'Two strange men came by when we were at the basketball court,' he found himself blurting out to his parents.

'Strange in what way?' asked Binti.

'You're not assuming they're smugglers by any chance?' Peter looked at him quizzically.

'None of Dario's friends had ever seen them before and they were in a bit of a hurry to get away from us,' Joe explained.

'I can understand that.' Peter grinned.

'They'll be visitors to the island, like us,' said Binti. 'This is such a small place, I expect we'll all bump into them before we leave.'

Joe hoped not. Whatever his parents said, he was sure the men were up to no good.

Chapter 10

The Brook family spent the next day lounging on the beach, resting ahead of their night-time sortie. Joe helped his father build an exotic sandcastle decorated with seaweed and shells, while Binti read and Aesha swam. Just before lunch, Rey appeared and took them for a practice snorkelling session around a rocky area at one end of the shoreline. Joe didn't find it easy, but was delighted by the brightly coloured fish he saw every time he put his face in the water.

'This is nothing,' Rey told him. 'You wait till we look in the big sea.'

In the afternoon, it was so hot that they sought

shade under a clump of trees and dozed fitfully, before returning to the staff house for dinner and then relaxing in their rooms.

They set out for the snorkelling trip at ten o'clock that evening. Much to Aesha's relief, the air was cooler as they meandered down the road towards the beach. This was the adventure Joe had been so looking forward to. There was something otherworldly about going out after dark in a country where all the sounds and sights and smells were so different from back home. Along the way, they passed houses lit by gas lamps and lanterns that cast eerie shadows across their path. Joe could hear laughter coming from them, and some of the islanders were sitting outside, chatting quietly, playing cards or simply meditating. The occasional grunt from a pig made him giggle, and the odd random scuffling in the undergrowth made him wish he had X-ray eyes so that he could see what was there.

As they walked on to the beach, Joe noticed a light glowing a few metres away.

'Rey's looking forward to showing you his world.' Angela chuckled. 'He's like a child anxious for you to love his favourite toy.'

'We can't wait to see his world,' said Binti. 'We're very privileged.'

They reached the *banca*, which now had a gas lamp attached to the front of it. Rey greeted them with big smiles and handed each of them a head torch.

'I show you the most beautiful place you ever go to,' he said.

They helped push the boat down to the sea and climbed in, Joe sitting as close to the gas lamp as he could, his flippers and snorkel across his lap, his head torch in place and his camera on the bench beside him. He began to get a little anxious as well as excited. *What if I get lost or can't snorkel well enough?* He didn't like the fact that with flippers on he couldn't put his feet down. It made him feel slightly panicky, especially when water got into his snorkel and all he wanted to do was stand up, pull off his mask and breathe in some air.

'Whatever you do, don't take off your flippers!' Angela had told them. 'If you tread on a sea urchin it's extremely painful.'

Joe focused his gaze on where the light from the gas lamp fell on the water. As the *banca* moved slowly away from the shore he could already see numerous shoals of small fish below the surface. He took his camera from its case and began to take photographs, the flash leaping into action with each shot.

'If any of your photos are good enough I'll use them in my article,' Peter promised.

Joe hoped they might be as he snapped a shoal of bright-eyed, silvery-mauve fish streaming alongside them. He looked back at the photograph on his screen and decided to call it 'Shadows under the Sea'.

They soon arrived at the marker buoys at the edge of the Marine Protected Area. Rey cut the *banca*'s engine and allowed the boat to drift while they put on their equipment and got ready to lower themselves into the water.

'Are you all right, Joe?' Binti asked him, slight concern in her voice.

Joe nodded. Excitement had quashed any fears he might have had and he could feel the adrenalin pumping through him now. The sea was incredibly calm, the sky cloudless and the moon nearly full. Fish were teeming close to the surface under the light from the gas lamp. Joe waited for his father and Aesha to dive in first, then sat with his legs over the side of the boat, his mask over his forehead, his head torch switched on, before slipping carefully into the water and turning on to his back. His flippered feet rose up in front of him, so that he wound up in a sitting position, where he had to paddle his arms furiously in order not to tip backwards.

'Stay close to Rey,' Angela called as she slipped into the water with Binti. 'He'll make sure you're safe and will show you where the seahorses are most commonly found.'

Rey dropped into the water last. To Joe's surprise, he wasn't wearing a snorkel, just a small pair of goggles carved out of wood, and he only had a home-made flipper on one foot.

'I find you the best place,' Rey said.

With that, he grabbed a rope that hung down from the front of the *banca*, took a deep breath, turned a somersault in the water and disappeared under the surface, pulling the boat along behind him so that the gas lamp lit his route. He resurfaced several metres away before plunging in again.

Joe pulled down his mask, bit on the mouthpiece of the snorkel, rolled on to his front and carefully lowered his face into the sea. He felt the gentle ripple of the waves as he waited for his eyes to focus. When they did, he was filled with wonder at what he saw. The shapes and colours of the reef were more extraordinary than anything he had seen in books or on television and the noise was almost deafening. It was like entering a garden created by someone from a different planet. Fish of every size and hue were flitting in all directions, stopping briefly to explore nooks and crannies for food. Bright red anemones waved their tentacles alongside deep-purple sea urchins. Orange starfish crept over yellow sponge-like corals. Joe recognised a lion-fish and followed its progress as it swam through crevices and willowy fronds. Then an enormous grey fish emerged just below him. He was so excited that he opened his mouth to call out – and immediately swallowed a large amount of briny water. Spluttering and choking, he rolled over to find Rey right next to him, grinning from ear to ear and holding a big crab.

'Sea not taste nice, eh? You like to stroke him?'

Joe looked doubtfully at the crab's huge pincers.

'Crab taste much nicer than sea.' Rey smiled.

He let the crab go, took hold of the rope and disappeared again. When at last he came back up, some distance away, he gestured to Joe's family to come and join him.

'Here,' he said. 'Seahorses.'

Chapter 11

The Brooks followed Rey as he tracked down several seahorses and related pipefish. Their guide even cupped one seahorse in his hand and gave it first to Aesha and then to Joe to hold. Joe was thrilled when the seahorse curled its black-and-yellow-striped tail round his finger.

'That's a tiger tail seahorse.' Angela took off her mask to inform them. 'They're so well camouflaged that only someone as experienced as Rey can spot them, even though they're bigger here than outside the Marine Protected Area.'

'He's so cute,' said Aesha. 'I can see why

people are tempted to keep them as pets, even though it's cruel.'

When Rey pointed out a pregnant male, its belly bulging and its partner close by, Joe thought it was one of the best things he had ever seen. He was fascinated by the way they anchored themselves on sponges and pieces of coral and swayed gently in the swell.

For an hour they explored the area where the seahorses were most abundant. Rey led them to other sea creatures as well and every few seconds something new came into view.

This is much more fun than watching television or playing computer games, Joe decided.

He was disappointed when the time came for them to return to the village.

'We can't stay out all night,' said Binti as they returned to the *banca*. 'Poor Angela and Rey have to work in the morning.'

'Can we do it again?' Joe asked.

'We'll see how the time goes,' said Peter. 'Rey will be going diving with me tomorrow so that I can take photos of the reef where it's deeper, but we can't expect him to miss his beauty sleep every night.'

Rey laughed out loud. 'Have to stay beautiful for my wife.'

'I think you'll need a quiet day tomorrow,' Angela said to Joe. 'I bet you won't be up as early as usual.'

Joe pulled a face. He was sure he would be, but he didn't want to argue in case it sounded rude. He still felt wide awake when they reached the shore, though he could feel the tiredness in his legs as they made their way back up to the staff house.

'It's surprising how much snorkelling takes out of you, isn't it?' said Binti, putting her arm round his shoulders as he began to trail behind everyone else.

'I'm all right,' he said, but when they reached their room and he lay down on the sleeping mat, he went out like a light.

Joe was woken by the sound of heavy rain. It was pitch black and he had no idea what time it was. He wanted to get up off his sleeping mat and look through the window, but he was worried about letting mosquitoes in under the net. He listened to the rain hammering on the nearby electricity generator and wondered how he would ever get back to sleep. He sat up and looked across at Aesha. She hadn't stirred and wouldn't, he was sure, even if someone were to explode a paper bag right by her ear.

He lay back and listened intently. The rain was torrential, drowning out almost every other noise, but he thought he heard the buzz of a motorbike, and wondered why anyone would be driving around on such a night. The effort of listening made him feel hot. He kicked the sheets away and strained his ears. Nothing. He closed his eyes.

The next time Joe woke, it was broad daylight and he found himself alone in the room. He leapt off his sleeping mat and ran to the window. It had stopped raining but the sky was heavy with clouds. He could hear voices coming from the thatched pavilion area and was cross with himself for oversleeping, especially knowing that Aesha was already up. *What time is it?* He dressed quickly and ran through the house, which was deserted.

When he reached the pavilion, he discovered that his family was there, as well as Angela, Rey, Carl and Dario. The table was covered in used glasses and plates and everyone looked sombre.

'Good afternoon,' his father said when he saw him.

Joe pouted. 'Why didn't you wake me up?'

'Aesha said you were sleeping like a baby.'

Joe glared at his sister. He felt embarrassed

with his new friend sitting there watching. 'I got woken up by the rain in the night,' he said defensively. 'Why is everybody looking so serious?'

'We've had word from the wardens that someone might have gone blast fishing in the night,' Angela told him. 'Carl's going to investigate, while Rey goes with your father so that he can take the photos he needs for his magazine.'

'Can I go too?' Joe asked eagerly.

'I'm afraid not,' said Peter. 'We're going to be diving today. It's time to get on with my assignment.'

'You can come with me,' said Dario. 'I show you other parts of the island – if it's OK?' He looked at Binti for approval.

'That's a great idea, isn't it, Joe? Aesha and I were thinking we might have another lazy day on the beach, so that would be perfect.'

Joe hesitated for a moment, unsure about spending the day away from his family, but quickly decided that it would be much more fun than sitting on the beach.

'How would you like to measure some of the mangrove trunks while you're at it?' Angela suggested. 'We need to start a new survey, so you could bring us our first results.'

Joe was doubtful at the prospect. Measuring mangrove trunks wasn't exactly what he had in mind, but Dario nodded enthusiastically and took charge of the tape measures and data sheets with great eagerness.

Chapter 12

Joe soon relaxed in Dario's company. There were so many things he wanted to ask him, and his new friend was happy to talk about his life on the island and his ambitions for the future. First of all he took Joe to his home to meet his mother and little brother. Joe was shocked by how tiny it was inside and couldn't imagine how they managed without electricity and running water. Dario's brother, who was only three, stared at Joe in wonderment, while his mother expressed her delight at having an English boy in her house.

'You take food with you. Boys always hungry,

I think,' she said, giving Dario some salted eggs, raisins and rice cakes to put in his rucksack. 'For *merienda*.'

'In English it is *snack*,' Dario explained.

'You speak good English,' said Joe.

'Our second language.' Dario grinned. 'You have second language?'

Joe pulled a face. 'I learn French in school, but I'm not very good at it. Mum's from Tanzania and can speak Swahili, but I only know a few words.'

They set off along a track towards the centre of the village, but then turned on to a paved path that took them through the village and ran parallel to the seashore. They passed the church that Joe had seen highlighted on the map and a short distance further on came to the school where Dario was a pupil.

'When Father was a fisherman and there was not enough fish we did not go to school because he did not have the money. Now he makes money from farming chickens and seaweed, and my mother, she sells bags and I can go to school and I'm happy.' Joe could see that Dario was proud to go to school.

'What do you want to be when you're older?' he asked.

'I will be a biologist,' Dario said with great certainty. 'And you?'

'A photographer, or a vet,' Joe replied. It prompted him to take out his camera and direct his friend to pose in front of the school. Dario obliged, but then demanded that Joe have his photograph taken as well.

'You pretend to be Filipino schoolboy,' he said, grinning.

They continued on their way, Joe stopping every so often to photograph snuffling pigs, squawking chickens and brightly coloured orchids. Dario begged Joe to take a photograph of him kneeling down next to one of the pigs, and they hooted with laughter when the owner came out and offered them a bowlful of slops. The sun was shining brightly as they left the village behind and headed for the countryside, still walking parallel to the seashore.

'Rain come later,' Dario told Joe, squinting up at the sky. 'Maybe big rain.'

Joe thought he would welcome the rain because it was threatening to be a sizzling hot day and he was already sweating profusely. He was looking forward to jumping in the water when they dropped down to the sea. On the way they stopped under the shade of a palm tree to eat the mangoes Binti had packed for them. Joe felt he could quite easily lie back and fall asleep, and was about to make himself comfortable when they heard the drone of an approaching motorbike. They gazed along the path as it drew closer. The motorbike was ridden by two men, who stared straight ahead as they sped past the boys. Joe realised with a jolt that they were the men from the basketball court. He said so to Dario, but again his friend didn't seem interested, much to Joe's disappointment.

When they finished their snack they carried on along the path. Joe wondered how much further they had to walk before they reached the mangroves. He was enjoying himself, but he was tiring quickly in the heat and his flip-flops were beginning to rub blisters between his toes. At last, Dario turned down a track that zigzagged through low-growing bushes in the general direction of the sea.

'Villagers replant big lot of trees in this place,' he told Joe. 'One time no trees are left because people use to make houses. Ma'am Angela, she helps people see that no trees is not good because land is washed away without them. We had much fun to plant the mangroves again. Lots of children helped.'

Joe nodded and thought he would have enjoyed helping. At least he was able to do his bit now by measuring the trees to see how much they had grown. He wondered whether he would have felt the same if someone had asked him to measure a few trees in England. *Probably not.* He grinned to himself. *But this is different.*

The vegetation around them began to change and muddy water seeped over the sides of Joe's flip-flops. The boys were greeted by a cacophony of birdsong. Joe pulled his camera out again and peered up through the treetops. He was hoping he might capture a fruit bat on film, but even the few sightings he made of birds were too brief for him to be able to zero in on them.

'The birds do not want to have a photo.' Dario laughed. 'They are shy!'

They reached the water's edge. Dario hung his rucksack on the branch of a tree and stripped down to his swimming shorts. Joe wasn't sure what to do with his camera, though. He wanted to keep hold of it in the event that there was something worth photographing, but that was impractical. Reluctantly, he hung it on another branch, before taking off his T-shirt and swapping his flip-flops for a pair of protective plastic sandals, in case there was anything nasty lurking on the seabed.

'Swim first, work after,' Dario said, smiling. 'Be careful where you are putting your feet.'

Joe gingerly tiptoed into the water. It became clearer and clearer the further away they moved from land, and he was intrigued to see the long, tangled roots of the trees stretching downwards into the muddy seabed, almost like an upside-down forest. Colourful sponges and anemones had attached themselves to the roots, while tiny crabs scuttled up and down and shoals of small fish flitted among them, all feeding on the organisms that had their homes there.

'Some of the roots are huge!' he called out to Dario.

'Old trees,' replied Dario, who was floating on his back. 'Some not cut down before.'

Joe turned over on to his back as well, flapping his feet to push himself away from the mangroves, enjoying the coolness of the water. Although the sun was beating down, black clouds were gathering on the horizon.

Chapter 13

After a while, Joe and Dario returned to the shore, tucked into their salted eggs, rice cakes and dried mango, then set about measuring the mangrove trunks. They stood shoulder deep in the water and each took one end of the tape measure, manoeuvring themselves round the trunks until they had an accurate record of their girths. Dario had been involved in previous surveys and knew exactly what to do. Occasionally, in order to circumnavigate a trunk, he lowered his snorkel mask over his face and disappeared below the surface of the water, re-emerging with a whoop on the far side. Joe wished he had brought his own snorkel with him, especially when Dario brought up first a prawn and then a huge starfish he had discovered.

'They are happy here,' Dario said, grinning. 'Mangrove is nursery for them.'

The sky was growing blacker all the time as they continued their work. Joe thought it wouldn't make much difference to them if it rained, but he was tiring from the effort of pushing through the water and holding up the tape measure, and it was becoming too dark to see what they were doing. At last, as the first drops of rain began to fall, Dario decided they should go back.

'Rain might be very big,' he said, and began to scramble on to the shore.

Just then there was a loud *whoosh* from somewhere not too far away. The sea began to eddy and churn. Joe tried to grapple his way on to firm ground, but a huge wave rolled towards him, washing over his shoulders and tugging at his legs. He found himself being sucked down to the seabed. He kicked and battled, gasping for breath. He felt himself being lifted again. Something caught one of his hands. He fought against it until he realised that it was Dario trying to haul him out.

'Hold on, Joe,' his friend called.

'Help me,' Joe cried when the sea dragged at him anew.

He gripped Dario's hand with all his might, terrified at one point that the boy would lose his balance and fall in with him. But as he held on, the turbulence gradually died down and he was finally able to crawl ashore. He rolled on to his back, exhausted. Only then did he notice the torrential rain, which drummed at his face and body.

'You OK?' Dario asked, squatting next to him.

Joe nodded. He was beginning to shake as it dawned on him that he'd had a very lucky escape. 'You saved my life,' he said. 'Thank you.' His voice sounded strangely disconnected and the words wholly inadequate. 'What happened?'

'Dynamite. Someone use dynamite to fish. I go find who. You wait for me.'

Joe took in what Dario said and panicked. 'I'm coming with you,' he asserted, struggling to his feet. 'I'm not staying here on my own.'

'There might be danger,' Dario cautioned. 'Those people not like to be caught.'

Joe hesitated, wondering what his friend intended to do, and then it came to him like a flash. 'It was those two men! I bet it was those two men!'

'What men?'

'The men on the motorbike. The same men we saw at the basketball court.'

All of a sudden, Joe was more excited than fearful. He held the clue as to who was carrying out the blast fishing, he was sure of it. If only he could remember exactly what they looked like.

'We don't know who it was,' said Dario, 'but we will see, I hope.'

He headed off through the trees, following the line of the shore. Joe ran after him.

'Go quietly,' Dario warned him.

It was raining so hard that the ground was beginning to flood. Muddy water splashed up Joe's legs and rain streamed down his face. He had no idea what Dario had in mind, but in his own head he wanted to confront the men and make them aware of the damage they were doing. *You're selfish and irresponsible, and you're destroying the planet,* he imagined himself saying to them. *Don't you care?* They might be dangerous, though, as Dario had said. Perhaps his friend just wanted to have a look at them so that he would be able to recognise them if he saw them again and then report them to the authorities. The best thing would be to take a photograph of them secretly and hand it to the police.

A photograph. *My camera!* In horror, Joe remembered he had left his camera hanging on the branch of a tree, out of its case. *It'll be wrecked!*

'My camera!' he called out to Dario, but the

older boy was too far ahead. Joe stopped in his tracks, desperate to go back and get it. At the same time, he didn't want to lose sight of Dario and miss out on what might happen with the men. Besides, Dario might need him.

'I see their boat,' Dario shouted back at him. 'They are fishing still.'

'I'm going to get my camera,' Joe cried determinedly. 'I might be able to photograph them.'

If Dario responded, Joe didn't hear him. He spun round and began to retrace the route they had taken, pushing tree branches aside and focusing solely on the odd footprint that confirmed he was going in the right direction. *Don't get lost!* he kept saying to himself. The rain was bouncing off the ground in front of him, gradually wiping out the footprints and blurring his vision. *Don't get lost!*

At last, he came to the place where they had dropped down to the water's edge. His camera was still hanging from the branch where he had left it, alongside Dario's rucksack. He grabbed them both, stuffing the camera into the rucksack and slinging the rucksack over his shoulders, and set off again.

With every step he grew more fearful that he might not reach his friend, that Dario might have thought he was going home. *What if something's happened to him?* Eventually, to his relief, he saw Dario in the distance, gesturing at him to hurry up.

'You scare me,' Dario said, when Joe caught up with him. 'I think you get lost and then Ma'am Angela and your parents will not be happy with me. Stay with me now.'

They pushed their way through dense, low-growing shrubs that took them nearer and nearer to the place where the two men would be likely to come ashore.

'I thought I could photograph the men as soon as they're close enough,' Joe tried to explain again.

'Then they will be too close,' said Dario. 'I have a better idea, I think.'

They came to the edge of a small clearing. In front of them, leaning against a clump of shrubs, was a motorbike. Joe's heart skipped a beat.

'I was right!' he said excitedly. 'It *was* those men we saw!'

Dario nodded. 'So now we catch them.' He grinned at Joe. 'You ever ride motorbike?'

Joe was amazed at the question. He shook his head. 'I'm too young,' he said.

'Not in front,' Dario explained. 'You sit behind, I sit in front. I know what to do. They leave the key in the engine. I can make it go.'

The full import of what Dario was suggesting hit him. All at once Joe felt exhilarated – and scared stiff.

Chapter 14

Dario positioned himself behind a large tree trunk and peered round it towards the sea. 'Keep by me,' he said to Joe. 'Be ready.'

Joe did as he was told. He couldn't see anything; being shorter, there were bushes obscuring his view. He was reliant upon Dario telling him what was going on.

'We wait until they don't face this way, then we run – quick – to the motorbike. We ride – very quick – to the village and we tell the village captain what we see so they come here and catch the men.'

Joe's heart was pounding now. *Dario's only*

thirteen. Am I really going to get on a motorbike with him? Has he ridden one before? Joe didn't think he had any choice. He was likely to get lost if he tried to walk back on his own, and the men might catch him, even though they would have no reason to concern themselves with him if they were unaware that he knew what they had been doing.

Dario grabbed his elbow. 'Now. We go now. Run!'

He sprinted over to the motorbike and pulled it away from the bushes. Joe dashed after him. Dario held it upright and told Joe to get on. As he obeyed, they heard shouts. Dario clambered on in front and tried to start the engine. Joe looked out to sea. The men were standing in their *banca*, waving furiously at them, but they were too far away to do anything. Joe turned back, feeling rather smug for a moment. He caught sight of a flash of red behind the trees. Before he could think what it might be, and as the motorbike engine roared into life, a man broke through the trees and came tearing towards them. Joe could see straight away that the man was angry. *He must be an accomplice!*

'Hurry!' he yelled.

Dario turned and saw the danger. He put his foot down on the accelerator and revved it hard. It spluttered and died, then spluttered again.

'He's closing on us!' Joe cried.

They began to move – too slowly on the soft ground, it seemed to Joe. He held on tight to his friend and prayed that they were out of reach of the man, whose voice seemed to come from right next to them.

At last the motorbike picked up speed. Joe looked round and saw the man running back through the trees, away from them. Out at sea the two men on the *banca* were frantically collecting the fish they had killed with the blast. Joe felt like waving tauntingly at them, but was too scared to let go of Dario, who was weaving precariously along the slippery unmade road.

'They'll never be able to catch us now!' he cried, in the hope that the older boy would slow down.

Dario couldn't hear him above the engine noise and kept his foot pressed hard on the accelerator. Joe looked round again. Just then, he saw the man reappear – on another motorbike. He dug Dario in the back.

'He's coming after us!' he yelled at the top of his voice.

Dario caught sight of the motorbike in his mirror. He leant forward, urging their motorbike to go faster, but it wasn't very powerful. The other motorbike was gaining ground on them with every turn of its wheels. Now Joe was really terrified. *What's he going to do to us?* He could almost feel the man breathing down his neck as the other motorbike rumbled up behind them. Dario turned to look. At that moment, their motorbike hit a pothole.

Joe found himself being thrown through the air. There was a screech of tyres and a sickening crunch of metal. Joe landed some distance away, his fall broken by scrubby plants. He lay there for a moment, winded, trying to make sense of what had happened. A bird was chirping some-where close by, but otherwise it was strangely quiet – until he heard footsteps scrabbling towards him. He sat bolt upright, fear hitting him like a blast from a shotgun.

'Are you all right, Joe?' His friend was there, a trickle of blood running down his face from a cut above his eye.

Joe nodded. 'I think so.'

'We must run,' Dario urged, pulling him to his feet.

The man shouted something incomprehen-sible and Joe saw their pursuer waving his fist at them.

'Quick!' said Dario. He shoved Joe in the direction of the woodland that lined the road.

Joe didn't need to be told twice. He ran as fast as his legs would let him, until he reached the first line of trees and slowed to look round.

The man must have set off after them, but had stopped and was making his way back to the wreckage on the road. Only then did Joe realise that after they had been thrown from their motorbike, the other motorbike had ploughed into it. It made him feel faint and he had to steady himself against the trunk of a tree. Dario stood beside him, breathing heavily, and Joe noticed that he had a deep gash in one of his shins.

'You're injured.' Joe pointed at Dario's leg.

'Now they have time to get away,' Dario said unhappily. 'Now they can do it again.'

'We did our best,' replied Joe. *We could have died!* he realised.

They watched ruefully as the man struggled to separate the two motorbikes. Joe fiddled absent-mindedly with the strap of Dario's rucksack and suddenly remembered what his father was always telling him: '*One of the secrets of being a successful photographer is being ready to snap when the unexpected happens.*' He didn't even know if his camera would still work after the treatment it had received, but it was worth a try.

Joe quickly removed the camera from the rucksack, pointed the lens at the man and took one shot after another. He even dared to creep a few steps closer, squatting down behind a bush, because he was worried the zoom might not be powerful enough for the photographs to be clear.

'Now let's go – quick,' said Dario. 'The village captain can still catch up with them.'

Joe put his camera away and hurried after Dario. As they raced along, he imagined how he would feel if it turned out that his camera contained the evidence to convict the rogues who were destroying the coral reef. *That would be so cool!*

Chapter 15

As luck would have it, when they felt safe enough to follow the road, a man from the village came by on his bike. Dario waved his arms, ran into the road and shouted at him to stop. He explained about the dynamite fishermen and begged the man to cycle on ahead of them, as fast as possible, to alert the people at the seahorse project to what had happened and to let them know that they were unharmed. The man agreed and set off again, pedalling earnestly. Joe was disappointed. He had been looking forward to breaking the news with Dario and seeing everyone's reaction, but he understood that speed was of the essence if there were to be any chance of catching the men red-handed.

'What do you think those men are doing now?' he asked Dario.

'They are not happy because those motor-bikes will not work.' He grinned at Joe.

'They were a bit of a mess,' Joe said soberly. 'Is your head all right, and your leg?'

Dario looked down. 'They will mend,' he replied. 'Those men not like to leave the fish behind. I think the village captain will catch them with the fish.'

Joe wished he could be there to watch, though a small part of him wanted the men to escape so that the evidence his camera held would be crucial. He was keen to tell his father about everything they had been through and how he had been ready to snap the unexpected. At the same time, he was worried about how his mother would react. She would be appalled that he had been in such danger – that he might have been killed. She would never want to let him out of her sight if she thought he was going to get himself into such trouble. He hoped he might be able to speak to Peter alone first and ask him to play the danger down to Binti.

'What will your mother say when she sees you?' he asked Dario.

Dario shrugged. 'She knows I can look after myself.'

Joe was sure Dario wouldn't tell his mother he nearly went under the wheels of a motorbike. *She wouldn't think he could look after himself if she knew that!*

The rain was becoming torrential again. They could scarcely see ahead, but some lights were shining through the trees and Joe was delighted to discover they had arrived back at Handumon. A wave of relief almost over-whelmed him. He felt his knees buckling at the thought that in a few minutes he would be safe with his family and someone else would be taking charge. He had wanted adventure, but what they had experienced was almost an adventure too far and he was exhausted. It seemed like a lifetime ago that they had set out along the road to the mangrove forests.

'Tired, Joe?' Dario asked, as though able to read his thoughts.

Joe nodded.

'I think you sleep like a baby tonight, and me too.'

They reached the staff house and entered the communal room. Everyone was gathered there. Joe could see from the look on Binti's face that she had been worried stiff about him.

'Two drowned rats!' Peter exclaimed, before spotting that Dario was bleeding.

Joe felt a desperate urge to cry, but bit his lip hard and resisted running to his mother for comfort.

'Go and fetch some towels,' Binti ordered Aesha, while Angela produced a first-aid kit and went to work on Dario's wounds.

'What on earth happened?' Peter asked.

'We got your message about the blast fishing,'

said Angela. 'The wardens are on their way and the village captain has been informed.'

Dario began to explain the sequence of events. Joe piped up every so often to add details that his friend had missed. He didn't want to frighten his mother, but at the same time, and now that they were safe, he was eager for the adults to understand how heroic he and Dario had been.

'And guess what, Dad,' he said finally. 'I took photos of the man who chased after us.'

Joe was pleased with the reaction. Even when he admitted that his camera had got very wet and could have been damaged and that the man hadn't been very close to them, he could tell his father was impressed, and Angela was hopeful it might contain crucial evidence.

'Shall we have a look now?' she suggested. 'I might recognise him.'

Joe took the camera out of the rucksack. He was concerned to see how wet it was and looked doubtfully at Peter. He opened up the screen and pressed to enter the image gallery. Nothing happened. He pressed again. This time a row of photographs appeared. He scrolled through the shots he had taken since they had arrived in the Philippines, until he came to the last few. It was impossible to disguise his dismay.

'It's too dark,' he said, scowling. 'You can't see anything.'

'Let me see,' said Peter.

Joe handed the camera over and went to sit with Binti. His father studied the photographs and announced that when the final shot was blown up, and with a few tweaks, they might well be able to make out the man's features.

'I'll do it tomorrow if I can borrow one of your computers,' he said to Angela.

Angela agreed that there was nothing else to be done until the morning, and thought they should wait until they had news from the wardens and the village captain.

'It's been a very long day for all of us,'

concluded Binti. 'I think we should eat and have an early night.'

They said their farewells to Dario, who turned to Joe as he parted and said, 'Next time you say you see strange men, I listen to you.'

Chapter 16

Joe slept soundly that night, just as Dario had predicted, even though the minute he relaxed on to his sleeping mat he discovered a number of bruises around his ribs that must have been caused by his fall from the motorbike. He dozed off trying to count them and wasn't aware of anything else, until his father gently shook his shoulder and asked if he was planning to stay in bed all day.

'We thought you might like to hear the news,' Peter said. 'It seems two of your strange men have been caught.'

Joe struggled up off the sleeping mat. 'What happened, Dad? How did they get caught?'

'Come and have breakfast and we'll tell you.'

Joe clambered awkwardly into his clothes. His body felt as if it had been used as a punchbag. He made his way to the pavilion, where everyone else had already gathered. Dario was there and Joe was shocked to see how his face had swollen up overnight.

'Hello, Joe. How are you feeling?' his mother asked, concerned.

'OK,' he said, sitting down next to her.

'Well, thanks to our two heroes here,' Angela announced, 'two of the men who carried out the dynamite fishing have been caught and are in custody.'

Joe was eager to know every detail and joined in the laughter when he heard what had transpired. It seemed that the two men in the *banca* had gone ashore to wait for their friend to return. When he failed to reappear, and determined that they were not going to lose their catch, they had had no option but to get back into the *banca* and try to make their escape by sea. It wasn't long before they ran out of fuel, and the wardens had no trouble rounding them up.

'But what about the other man?' Joe asked.

'It seems he's done a runner,' Angela replied. 'The motorbikes were found abandoned, and he may well have left the island by now.'

Joe was dismayed. 'So my photo won't be any help.'

'Oh yes it will,' said Angela.

'We're going to work on it,' Peter explained. 'If we can sharpen it up enough to provide an identifiable image, it can be sent to all the wardens and the authorities, not just here but on the neighbouring islands as well, and they'll add him to their files and keep a lookout for him.'

Joe was thrilled. 'Cool!' he said. 'My photo might be used to catch a criminal!'

'I think you might just want to look at the photos I took yesterday,' Peter added, 'but I'm obviously going to have to watch out, or you'll soon be taking over from me!'

In all the events of the day before, Joe had completely forgotten that his father had gone out photographing seahorses. He was eager to see the results. He followed him into the communal room and sat down next to him at the computer.

'I'll show you my videos and photos first,' said Peter, 'and then we'll get to work on your man.'

The world that opened up to them as he moved from one frame to the next was even more beautiful and extraordinary than Joe remembered it from the snorkelling trip. In an ever-changing landscape of smooth-domed rocks and intricately shaped corals, the creatures of the sea seemed to dance and sail and sway as if to the strains of music from an unseen piper. Then there were shots of seahorses taken from all angles, some of them clinging to coral with their tails, others peeping out from behind coral stems as though playing hide-and-seek. Joe was enchanted.

'All of this will have been destroyed in the area where those men set off their dynamite, and it won't recover for a very, very long time,' Angela observed sadly.

'Before we leave tomorrow, I'd like to photograph what they've done so that I can show it to the world alongside these photos,' said Peter. 'I'm sure the magazine I'm working for will agree that this should be publicised.'

He turned his attention to Joe's photograph of the man with the motorbike. Joe watched as he uploaded the image and zeroed in on the man's face.

'Nobody will be able to recognise him from that,' Aesha said rather dismissively.

'You wait and see,' said Peter. 'You'll be surprised what you can do with the right software.'

They watched intently as he manipulated the photograph. Gradually, a sharper image began to appear, whose features became more obvious by the minute, until at last Joe was able to say,

'That's him! That's absolutely him! I can see his big nose!' He looked to Dario to confirm that the likeness was now obvious.

'We don't like this man,' Dario said grimly. 'He is not a nice man.'

'The most important thing that I've spotted is that he has a very large ring on the little finger of his left hand,' said Peter.

'And a gap between his front teeth!' cried Joe. 'I remember it from when he shouted at us.'

'I'm horrified at the thought of what might have happened to you both,' said Binti, squeezing Joe's arm. 'You had a very lucky escape.'

Joe was glad that Angela stopped his mother from dwelling on what could have happened by sharing her thoughts.

'There's nothing the man can be charged with if we do come across him because we don't have enough evidence of his involvement, but at least now he'll know that we're on to him and it might make him think twice about a repeat performance. We'll be posting his mugshot far and wide, not just in the hope that someone will recognise him, but also as a warning that we'll be hot on the heels of anyone who tries the same thing.'

Joe felt his chest swelling with pride. He was sad to be moving on from this island where he'd had such an amazing adventure – not to mention a close escape from very real danger. But he would be leaving behind a photograph he had taken, a photograph that would be used to help protect the fascinating yet fragile underwater world he had been privileged to explore. How cool was that!

Zoological Society of London

ZSL London Zoo is a very famous part of the
Zoological Society of London (ZSL).

For almost two hundred years, we have been
working tirelessly to provide hope and a
home to thousands of animals.

And it's not just the animals at ZSL's Zoos in
London and Whipsnade that we are caring for.
Our conservationists are working in more than
50 countries to help protect animals in the wild.

To help save seahorses, we co-founded Project Seahorse,
which is making real progress towards protecting these
incredible animals from overfishing and habitat loss.

But all of this wouldn't be possible without your help.
As a charity we rely entirely on the generosity of our
supporters to continue this vital work.

By buying this book, you have made an essential
contribution to help protect animals.
Thank you.

Find out more at **zsl.org/projectseahorse**

Turn the page for a taster of Joe's exciting
adventures in the realm of the Amur tiger in

Paw Prints in the Snow

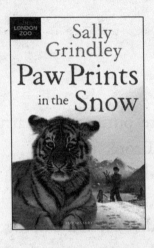

Joe and his family are in Russia on the trail
of one of the world's rarest creatures,
the beautiful Amur tiger.

Exploring a vast, freezing nature reserve,
Joe comes closer to the tigers than he ever
imagined – and is drawn into a daring
mission to rescue an injured cub . . .

Chapter 1

'What's it like putting your arm up a cow's bottom?' Joe Brook asked.

'Warm and squelchy.' Binti, his mother, grinned.

'You wouldn't catch me doing it.' Joe pulled a face.

He was standing on the bottom rung of some metal fencing inside a barn on Mike Downs's farm. His mother was the other side of the fence, dressed in her green overalls and wellington boots, her breath coiling upwards like steam from a kettle as she leant against the cow's rear. Joe watched as she pulled her arm out and removed the long plastic glove that covered most of it.

'It's not much fun for the cow, either,' she said.

'If I was going to be a vet, I'd only want to look after small animals like cats – or wild animals like elephants, because that would be cool.'

'So you think some of what I do is cool then, Joe?'

Binti smiled as she opened the gate and left the cow's enclosure. Most of her work was as an international wildlife vet, but when she was at home she sometimes helped out if called upon by other vets in the area.

'You might have to put your arm up an elephant's bottom too, you know,' she said.

'What for?'

'To find out if a female is pregnant, or perhaps to check for digestive problems. Pretty much the same as for a cow.'

'Well, I wouldn't mind so much if it was an elephant, because they're exciting and I'm half Tanzanian. Cows are boring.'

'Not to a bull they're not.' Binti laughed as she scrubbed her hands. 'Come on, it's dinner time.'

'I'm glad Dad does the cooking, knowing where your hands have just been.' Joe smirked.

His mother cuffed him gently.

Joe shivered as they left the barn. It had become dark and very chilly. They headed back towards the farmhouse, where Mike Downs greeted them on the doorstep. Through a window Joe could see a fire burning brightly and wished he were sitting in front of it.

'I can't find anything abnormal, Mike,' said Binti, 'but I'll send a stool sample off to the lab and see if they come up with anything. In the meantime, just keep an eye on her and give me a call if you're at all worried.'

'Thanks, Binti. I'll try not to disturb your weekend any further.'

'It's all part of the job, Mike. We can't expect animals to fall sick only on weekdays.'

'Are you going to follow in your mum's

footsteps when you're older, young man?' The farmer winked at Joe.

'My son doesn't like getting his hands dirty, do you, Joe?' Binti smiled. 'Right, we ought to make a move. Bye, Mike.'

She linked her arm through Joe's. They walked quickly over to their four-by-four and clambered in.

'Turn the heating up, Mum,' said Joe. 'It's got really cold.'

Binti switched on the engine and played with the dials. 'You'll have to get used to the cold where we're going,' she said, shooting him a glance to watch his reaction.

Joe looked puzzled. 'We're going home for dinner, aren't we?'

'But what about when you break up for half-term?' Binti questioned.

Joe detected a whiff of excitement. 'I know,' he said. 'We're going to Antarctica!'

'Not quite,' said Binti. 'But we *are* going to Russia.'

'Russia?' Joe wasn't sure how to react. 'Why are we going to Russia?'

'I'm going to help train some of the young vets over there in how to anaesthetize tigers.'

'But there aren't any tigers in Russia, are there?' said Joe. 'I thought they were all in India and Sumatra.'

'There are Amur tigers in Russia. They're the biggest, and there are very few left.'

Russia had sounded like a boring place to spend half-term – until Binti mentioned tigers. Now Joe couldn't think of anything better, even if it was going to be cold . . .

OUT NOW